LOVE YOUR NEIGHBOR

Library of Congress Cataloging-in-Publication Data

Dobrin, Arthur, 1943–
    Love your neighbor / by Arthur Dobrin; illustrated by Jacqueline Rogers.
        p.   cm.
    Summary: A collection of thirteen stories featuring animal characters and lessons about life.
    ISBN 0-590-04410-9
    1. Children's stories, American. [1. Animals—Fiction.   2. Conduct of life—Fiction.
3. Short stories.] I. Rogers, Jacqueline, ill. II. Title. III. Series.
PZ7.D6612Lo   1999
[E]—dc21   97-44212
                                                                                                        CIP
                                                                                                         AC

12 11 10 9 8 7 6 5 4 3 2   9/9 0/0 01 02 03 04

Printed in Mexico   49
First printing, March 1999

LOVE YOUR NEIGHBOR

STORIES OF VALUES AND VIRTUES

BY ARTHUR DOBRIN

ILLUSTRATED BY
JACQUELINE ROGERS

SCHOLASTIC INC.
New York Toronto London Auckland Sydney

For MacKenzie and Ryan,
who have made my heart fuller than ever
— A.D.

For Nettie
— J.R.

A Note to Parents

For thousands of years, people have used fables as an entertaining way to teach a lesson. Sometimes, as in *Aesop's Fables*, the moral of the tale is obvious. Other times, the lesson is subtle. Indeed, some fables are best understood with time; they need to steep and are most meaningful when savored slowly. The fable simmers and then the point becomes clear suddenly—as a revelation—and the listener says, "Aha, I get it!"

The stories in *Love Your Neighbor* are about friendship, loyalty, and love. There are tales about stubbornness and prejudice, tolerance and being different. There are stories about growing up, living by one's convictions, and leaving home. And there are tales about freedom, lending a helping hand, and our relationship to the earth. Each ends with a thought-provoking question, rather than a moral, that is intended to invite discussion about the moral issues posed by the story and its characters.

Encourage your child to talk about the stories and characters. However hard it may be, resist the temptation to give your interpretation of the tales.

Being able to parrot the moral of a story doesn't mean that the child understands the concept behind the words. Also, a young child may draw conclusions different than an adult. Perhaps the child hasn't matured enough to understand the deeper meaning. Or maybe he or she has seen something that you haven't.

Adults can be most helpful by asking open-ended questions, such as, "What did you like about this story?" "Do you think the story teaches us anything?" or "Do any of the characters remind you of someone you know?"

Remember, the stories are meant to be enjoyed first. When children like a story, they eventually come to understand it. Once understood, the story will become their own and it will hold that much more meaning for them.

—Arthur Dobrin

Table of Contents

LOVE YOUR
NEIGHBOR

The Kindness of Squirrels

From the day they were born, Harley and Indiana were loyal friends. The two young squirrels played from sunup to sunset. They chased each other around the playgrounds, up and down trees, and across the roofs of houses. They sat side-by-side and talked about nothing in particular. They just loved each other's company.

"Here's what I think," Harley said one day to his companion as he gave her a kernel of popcorn.

"And what's that?" Indiana asked.

"When we grow up," Harley said, "I think we should build our homes near one another so we can remain friends forever."

Indiana twitched her nose in approval.

"Yes, indeed," she said.

Not long after, the day came for the two squirrels to leave their parents' nests. Harley gathered twigs and leaves and, with Indiana's help, built his new home in the woods. Indiana then built her house nearby.

Then one day, Harley told Indiana that he had fallen in love with Myrtle and was going to marry her.

"I'm so happy for you," Indiana said. And when Harley's wife had a litter of baby squirrels, Indiana became their godmother. On Tuesdays she went to their house and on Saturdays they went to hers. Every Sunday they all went to a cafeteria where the children had pizza and the adults drank strong coffee from small cups.

Indiana didn't want to marry. She lived happily in her house by herself, content to feed her fish, fix lawn mowers, and take brisk walks early in the morning.

True to their promise, Harley and Indiana remained fast friends.

One night as Indiana lay curled in her bed of leaves, she thought about her old friend and said to herself, "Harley has such a big family to care for while I only have myself to feed. So I'll take some of what I've saved for myself and give it to him."

That night, all was dark when Indiana quietly, secretly carried the food from her barn to Harley's. She opened the door and, without a squeak, left her gift on the floor.

At that moment, Harley woke with a start.

He turned to Myrtle and said, "Indiana has no one to help her with her work while we have our children to help us. We have more food than we need. I'm going to give her some."

"That's a good idea, dear," his wife said as she dreamily rubbed her eyes.

Harley jumped out of bed and went to his barn. Filling his cheeks with seeds and nuts, he silently scampered through the lanes and secretly left his stash in Indiana's barn.

This scurrying in the dark continued night after night—Indiana going to Harley's place and Harley going to Indiana's.

Only after the squirrels grew old and
died did others discover the secret Indiana and
Harley had kept from each other. The town's squirrels were
so moved by Harley's and Indiana's gift-giving that they built
a monument to honor them. Today, halfway between their houses,
stands a statue of the two small animals. An inscription on the
statue reads: For the kindest and most generous squirrels, the two
friends, Harley and Indiana.

**Harley and Indiana helped each other without telling each other.
Why do you think they decided to keep this a secret?**

For the
kindest and
most generous
Squirrels
the two friends
Harley
and
Indiana

Boris, Natasha, and the Giant Beet

Natasha and her husband Boris loved beets. They ate beets for breakfast, for lunch and dinner, and even for late night snacks. The two ostriches loved beets and beets and more beets.

One day they saw an advertisement in a gardening magazine.

"Look at this, Boris," Natasha said to her husband. "There is a seed that will produce the largest and sweetest beet imaginable."

"Let's get it!" Boris cried.

When the seed arrived, the husband and wife planted it carefully in their garden. As promised, the beet did grow bigger than any they had ever planted.

"My gosh, wife!" Boris shouted as he looked at the flourishing vegetable.

"This is the largest beet I've ever seen," Natasha said. "My mouth is watering already!"

By the end of spring, the beet took up nearly half the garden. By summer, it had grown even bigger. By autumn, Natasha decided that the beet was ready to harvest.

She went to the garden to pull it from the ground. She pulled and pulled, but the beet wouldn't come loose. It was so big that it just sat there — plump, juicy, mouthwatering, but very stubborn.

Then Boris tried to pull out the beet, but he was no more successful than was his wife. So they went to the garden together. Boris clutched the huge vegetable and Natasha held on to her husband. They yanked and they pulled, but nothing happened.

"This beet is laughing at us," Boris said. So they called their dog.

"Woody, would you help us pull this stubborn beet from the ground?" Natasha asked the Saint Bernard.

"Of course!" Woody agreed.

So Woody grabbed Natasha who grabbed Boris and
the three of them pulled together. But the beet would not move.

"This beet is still laughing at us," Natasha complained. She called Petrova.

"Would you please help us pull this beet from the ground?" she asked her
favorite pussycat. Petrova consented.

So Petrova held on to Woody who held on to Natasha who held on to
Boris and they all pulled. But the beet still would not move.

"We'll never pull this from the ground," Woody growled in his grumbly
voice.

"How will we ever enjoy this scrumptious beet?" Petrova wanted to know.

Just then Stanislas, the gerbil from next door, came along.

"We're having a problem," Petrova explained. "Would you please help us?"

"Do you really think that someone so small can make a difference?"
Natasha wondered.

"I don't know how much help I will be," the gerbil said. "But I'm willing
to give it a try."

So Stanislas grabbed Petrova who grabbed Woody who grabbed Natasha
who grabbed Boris. They pulled with all their might.

"*Uuuggh!*" they cried.

They pulled again.

"Mmmmph!" they moaned.

Suddenly the beet came out with a *whoosh*. Boris and Natasha and Woody and Petrova and Stanislas all got up from where they had fallen. It was the largest, most fabulous, most wondrous beet anyone had ever seen.

There was a feast that night. The family ate boiled beets and fried beets and mashed beets and drank juice made from crushed beets. But best of all they enjoyed borscht, a sweet red soup made with beets, sour cream, and green onions.

For days after, they ate the borscht both hot and cold. They sat at the table telling tales of the sweetest, most delectable vegetable anyone had ever eaten. They spoke with smiles on their faces — faces stained red from the juice of the one giant beet.

Everyone has something to offer. How do you think everyone in this story helped?

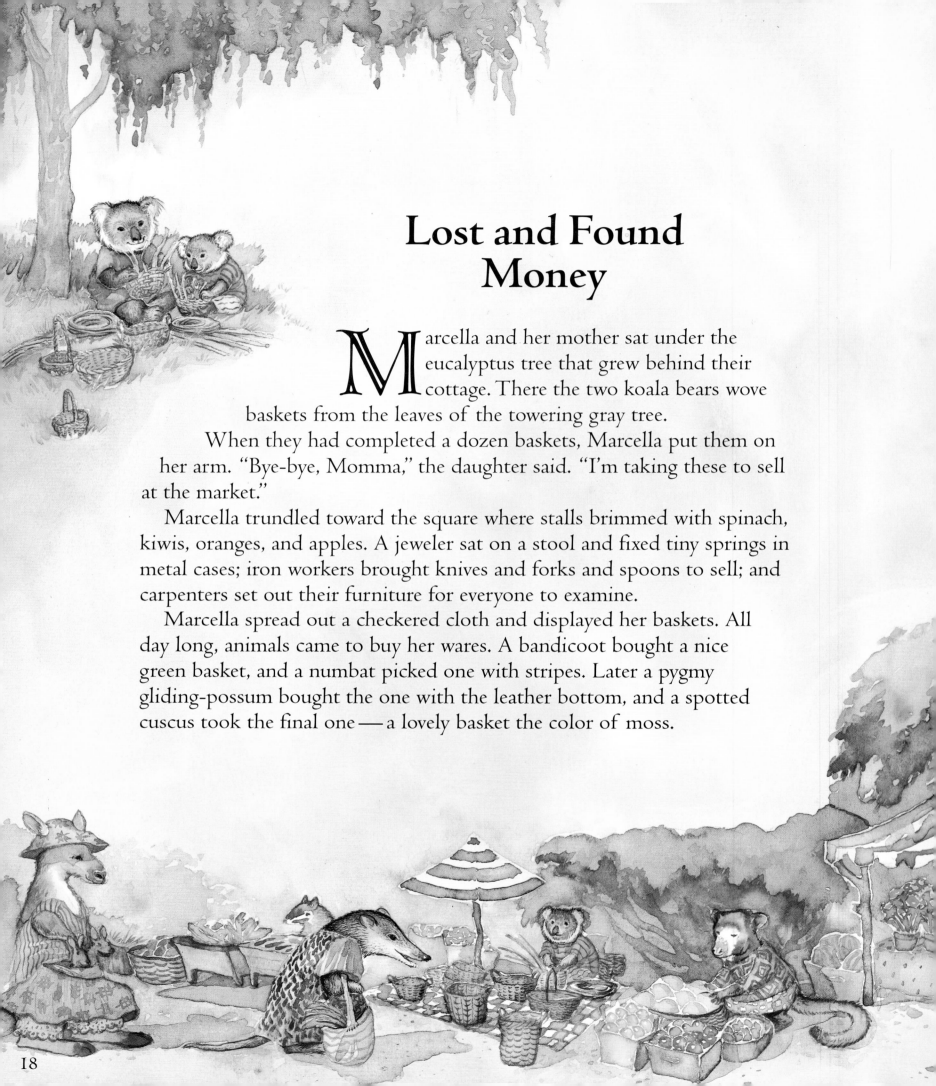

Lost and Found Money

Marcella and her mother sat under the eucalyptus tree that grew behind their cottage. There the two koala bears wove baskets from the leaves of the towering gray tree.

When they had completed a dozen baskets, Marcella put them on her arm. "Bye-bye, Momma," the daughter said. "I'm taking these to sell at the market."

Marcella trundled toward the square where stalls brimmed with spinach, kiwis, oranges, and apples. A jeweler sat on a stool and fixed tiny springs in metal cases; iron workers brought knives and forks and spoons to sell; and carpenters set out their furniture for everyone to examine.

Marcella spread out a checkered cloth and displayed her baskets. All day long, animals came to buy her wares. A bandicoot bought a nice green basket, and a numbat picked one with stripes. Later a pygmy gliding-possum bought the one with the leather bottom, and a spotted cuscus took the final one — a lovely basket the color of moss.

Marcella was exhausted from all the talking, all the showing, all the haggling over the proper price to be paid. As she leaned over to fold her checkered cloth, she saw a small bundle that she hadn't seen before.

"What is this?" she wondered as she untied the package. Marcella couldn't believe her eyes. Here was $50! This was more money than she had ever seen before. She wanted to tell someone what she had found, but the sun was almost down and everyone had gone by then.

Marcella ran all the way home and proudly explained how she had found the bundle on the ground.

"You know you didn't earn this money," her mother said. "So we will return to the market first thing tomorrow to find the rightful owner."

The next day the two koalas walked back to the market. Before they had a chance to begin their search, they met a wombat who was asking if anyone had found some money.

"Oh, I have," Marcella said, holding out the $50. She was happy to have discovered the owner of such a large sum of money. She thought he must have been very sad to have misplaced it.

The wombat, who was dressed in a fine silk shirt and wore a most expensive fedora, looked at the money in Marcella's paw.

"That's not what I lost," he said. "I lost twice that much—$100. Where is the rest of it?"

"But that's all I found," Marcella explained. She felt frightened as the wombat glowered at her.

"I want all of my money back," the wombat continued. He wiped his brow with a starched pawkerchief.

"It really is all I found," Marcella said, her voice getting smaller and smaller.

"You are a dishonest little girl," said the wombat as he wagged his manicured claw in front of her nose.

"Now, wait a minute," Marcella's mother interrupted. "My daughter is only trying to help return the money to its owner."

Everyone in the market gathered around out of curiosity. The wombat continued his accusations and Marcella no longer knew what to say.

Then a voice came from the crowd. "This is no way to settle a dispute." A kangaroo stepped forward. "I'm a judge, so let me decide what is fair."

"Yes, yes, let her decide what is fair," everyone agreed.

So the kangaroo questioned Marcella.

"I believe you," the kangaroo said. "Now let me hear from your mother."

"It is as she says," Marcella's mother added. "She came home with $50, not $100, your honor."

When it came time for the wombat to give his story, he swore that he lost $100 and the koala owed him the entire amount, not the half she said she found.

The kangaroo listened carefully and thumped her tail on the ground as she turned the matter over in her mind.

"Here's my decision," the kangaroo finally said. "I believe you are both telling the truth."

"They are both telling the truth?" the crowd murmured, confused.

"But since you, sir, lost $100 and the koala found only $50, the money she found cannot be yours. Therefore, she gets to keep the $50 and you will have to look elsewhere for your money."

The wombat began to sputter. Then he adjusted his hat and pushed his way through the crowd.

The gathering let out a little roar and then a round of laughter.

"Come on, Momma," Marcella said. "Let's buy some berry ice cream."

Marcella offered to buy a cone for the judge, but the kangaroo refused.

The two koalas returned home and played cards half the night, wondering what they were going to do with their newfound treasure.

We all find things at one time or another. What do you think Marcella should have done with the money?

21

First Flight

"Today is my day," Duncan said. "I am ready now to gather nectar like the grown-ups." He whirled his wings in a blur of speed. He zipped from one room to the other. "Yes. I am ready. I know I am!"

Duncan's mother, Mrs. Mellifera, buzzed with excitement.

"I think you're right," she said proudly. "You are a big boy now. You have bumbled around the hive long enough."

Duncan flew eagerly to the open window.

"Wait a minute, dear," his mother cautioned. "Don't go just yet. I've made something for you to wear."

The queen bee reached into a drawer and pulled out six woolen booties.

"I've knitted these to keep your feet warm," she said. "They'll look so nice on you."

"Oh, Ma," Duncan groaned. "Do I have to?"

His mother patted him on his hairy head. Duncan put on the socks and zipped to the front door.

"Wait!" Mrs. Mellifera called. "Put on your overcoat."

"Oh, Ma," Duncan complained. The little bee struggled with the heavy jacket that was as long as he was. His mother adjusted the collar and buttoned all the buttons.

"*Now* can I go?" Duncan asked.

"Just put this on," his mother added, placing a cap on her son's antennae. "And this," she said as she tied a muffler around his neck. "And this." She reached for a pair of earmuffs and placed them snugly over the top of the cap.

"Now can I go?" the young bee pleaded.

"Yes, you can go," Mrs. Mellifera said. "I think you'll be warm enough now."

Mrs. Mellifera watched as Duncan leaped into the air. He weaved and wobbled as he flew out the front door, then disappeared around the sycamore tree.

"Be back soon," his mother called, waving good-bye to him.

Unfortunately, Duncan didn't return
at the time he was expected. One hour passed,
then two. His mother began to worry.

"Oh dear, oh dear," Mrs. Mellifera fretted. "I hope my
little bee isn't lost. I should have told him to be careful."

Mrs. Mellifera stifled her tears and, without even putting on
a jacket herself, dashed from the hive to find Duncan. She hadn't gone
more than several yards past the sycamore tree when she saw Duncan
lying on the ground.

"Mom!" he called. "Help me. I can't get up."

Mrs. Mellifera nearly cried with relief at finding her son.

"What happened to you, Duncan?" she asked, her voice full of concern.
"Why are you on the ground?"

Duncan mumbled through his thick scarf. "I fell."

"I thought you knew how to fly," Mrs. Mellifera said as she helped him up.

"I do," he explained. "I fell because my clothes are too heavy. I can't move
my wings, my antennae are stuck in my hat, and all this weight has pulled
me down."

"Oh dear," she sighed. "All those clothes — whatever was I thinking?"

So with his mother's help, Duncan removed his earmuffs and hat, his
overcoat, his woolen muffler, and all six yellow-and-black booties.

"That's so much better," he sighed as he stretched his wings.

"Duncan," his mother said to him softly. "Please do me one favor."

"Sure, Ma," Duncan replied. "What is it?"

"Will you wear your cap when you go out? Then I will be able to see you when you are far away."

Duncan smiled at his mother.

"I can do that," he said. Then he flew figure-eights and headed for a meadow of scented flowers.

From that day on, Duncan flew from flower to flower with great speed and grace. He always carried lots of nectar for making golden honey. Still, his mother watched from the window. She always tried to see Duncan's red-and-blue cap dancing across the meadow far, far away.

Parents often worry about their children. Why do you think Duncan's mother had him wear so many clothes?

Love Your Neighbor

Isa lived in a lovely hutch in farm country. It was warm in the winter and the roof kept the rooms dry on rainy days.

On the other side of the split-rail fence lived Kobo who, unfortunately, wasn't as well-off as his neighbor. Kobo's burrow was tiny, but he thought of it as cozy. While it wasn't exactly the warmest place to spend cold evenings, he felt it was good enough for him.

Day after day, the two rabbits went to their fields to work. Isa worked the soil diligently. Luckily for him, his garden was very fertile. His lettuce sprouted large green leaves and his carrots were as big as baseball bats.

Kobo's ground wasn't so fertile. It was slightly sandy and full of rocks. No matter how hard he worked, Kobo managed to grow only enough to get by. His lettuce leaves were small and his carrots looked more like shriveled pickles.

One day Isa went looking in his barn for an ax to cut down an overgrown bush. When he opened his toolbox, he found his hammer, his screwdriver, his nails, and his pliers. But his ax wasn't anywhere to be found. It was gone!

Isa thought for a second.

"I know where that ax is," he said. Since Isa had a suspicious nature, he was certain that Kobo had taken his ax. Of course, Isa had no proof of this. Nevertheless, he was certain that his neighbor was a thief.

As Isa worked, he looked across his field to spy on his neighbor. Whenever he saw Kobo, he became more convinced that he was right.

"That rabbit has the look of a thief," Isa muttered. "Why, he hops like a thief. He holds his head like a thief. And his hands . . . "

"Hello, Isa," Kobo called to him.

Isa grumbled a reply.

"Hmm," he said to himself. "He even talks like a thief."

Shopping Spree

"Hi, Bubba," Ulu the Tabby purred into the telephone. "I'm going shopping. "Why don't you come along with me? I always want your advice."

"Sure, Ulu," Bubba the Burmese said to his friend as he licked his neat fur.

That afternoon the two cats met at Feline's Basement Mall. They padded up and down the crowded shopping mall: Ulu, orange and white and looking as though she had just come out of a washing machine, and Bubba, neat and stately.

"What do you want to buy?" Bubba asked.

"Oh, I'm not sure," Ulu replied. "If something strikes me, I'll know."

The two stepped into a clothing store.

"Do you like this?" Ulu asked as she came out of the dressing room. She was wearing a long black dress with a big white bow.

Before Bubba could answer, Ulu ran back into the dressing room and came out in jeans and a white T-shirt. "How about this?" she asked.

Bubba couldn't speak a word before Ulu had gone back to the dressing room and changed again.

"Me oh my," Ulu meowed as she came out wearing her latest outfit: a skirt with plastic beads and shiny silver bells. "This one is exactly right." Ulu turned around and around in front of the mirror and admired herself.

"If you think so," Bubba said, although he would never wear beads and bells himself.

Ulu wore her new skirt and the two friends continued on until they reached a shoe store.

"Do you like these?" Ulu asked as she first put on sandals, then high-heeled sneakers and, finally, yellow fisherman's boots.

"Well, I'm not so sure," Bubba responded, scratching his head.

"They will look divine with my new skirt," she said as she pawed through a pile of clothes on a counter. "And so will this!" She pulled out a polka dot vest and bought it at once.

Next the friends stopped at a jewelry booth.

"I love these," Ulu said as she hung a pair of sardine can earrings from her ears. She bought amber sunglasses and a necklace made of copper wire.

After lunch Ulu decided to get her hair cut. The barber held up pictures of one hairdo after another.

"I like this one," Ulu remarked, pointing to the one that most pleased her. Bubba put his paws in front of his eyes as electric scissors buzzed close to his friend's skin, leaving a pile of fur on the floor. What little hair remained on Ulu's head stood upright like fresh blades of spring grass.

"And dye it green, please," she said to the barber.

As Bubba looked at his friend, he couldn't help but smile.

"Why, Ulu," Bubba said, trying to find the right words. "You look, you look — just marvelous."

"Thank you, Bubba," Ulu purred. "I knew I could count on you to help me with my shopping. Do you think that I have everything now?"

"You have a skirt, boots, a vest, jewelry, sunglasses, and a great hairdo," Bubba replied. "But I think you're missing just one thing more."

Bubba took Ulu to a hat store. "I think this blue beret would look beautiful on you."

"No way," Ulu protested. "I won't wear a hat!"

"You won't?" Bubba said in surprise. "Why not?"

"Be serious, Bubba. Everyone would look at me," Ulu said sincerely.

Bubba smiled. He never liked his friend more than he did at that moment. He put his paw on Ulu's shoulder and licked her forehead.

"Yes," he said. "You're right. I think they would."

"But I think this would look great on you," Ulu told her friend and she bought a smart-looking cap for Bubba. The friends returned home, tired but happy with their new purchases.

Friends can be different from one another. What do you think Bubba liked about Ulu?

Chopsticks

Rhonda ate all day. She ate under a cloudless sky. She ate when it thundered and poured. Even when she slept, she dreamed of eating and eating some more. Like all the hippos she knew, Rhonda ate with chopsticks.

One day, while skipping beside the blue lake, Rhonda opened her red mouth and let out a song so loud that her rippling hippo fat shook and trembled.

"Dada da da da dada da da," she sang. Rhonda prepared for a dive. She kicked her legs together and flung her body with such joy that water flew into the air and descended like a rainstorm on her wide back.

Then Rhonda sat down, picked up her chopsticks, and slurped the green algae she gathered from the lake bottom.

"What are you doing, child?" asked Omogaka, an older hippo.

"I am eating," she said, "and having a grand old time."

"I know you are eating," Omogaka said, "but you've gotten it all wrong. The chopsticks should be held between your first and third toe, not your second and fourth."

"This is the way I do it," Rhonda explained. "I don't know another way."

"You must hold your chopsticks the proper way, so you can be a proper hippo," Omogaka said. "Here. I'll show you." He took out his pair of chopsticks and showed Rhonda what to do. She followed his instructions exactly, but it didn't feel right. The chopsticks fell, and with them, her food. She tried to pick up the food from the ground, but she could not.

"Keep at it," Omogaka said to Rhonda. "You will get it right."

When the older hippo returned to the lakeside several weeks later, he hardly recognized Rhonda. This wasn't the same hippo he had left, a singing and shaking hulk of a body. Instead of a fat, happy hippo, there sat a sad, skinny Rhonda.

"I'm so glad you've come back," Rhonda said in a whisper. She barely had the strength to talk. "I'm so hungry. I've had nothing to eat for weeks."

"What's the problem?" Omogaka asked.

"No matter how hard I try," she said, "I can't pick up my food. The algae keeps slipping and I keep dropping my chopsticks."

The older hippo thought for a moment.

"All the hippos here use their first and third toes," he said. "But I've been to other lakes where they use their second and fourth toes, just as you do. And now that I think about it, you are as proper as they are."

Rhonda's small ears twitched, her round eyes lit up, and she gave a little smile. She picked up her chopsticks and swallowed the slimy, wet algae as fast as she could.

And to this day, no one at Rhonda's lake eats the way she does. But no one cares, for they enjoy hearing her sing, *"Dada da da da dada da da."* Her body quakes and quivers, it shakes and shivers, and she splashes water that falls on her back like refreshing summer rain.

Some things can be done more than one way. Why do you think Omogaka changed his mind about the proper way to hold chopsticks?

Who Owns the Earth?

Between Gray Eagle Cliff and High Mountain is a broad valley filled with wildflowers and fruit trees. Birds and butterflies once flew about, but no animal lived on the land.

One day Matokuwapi, a large elk, looked down into the valley.

"This is where I want to live," he said.

Across the way, Tatanka, another elk, looked down at the land.

"I will live there," he said. "From this day on, I claim this land as my own!" he called out.

"I'm afraid you're mistaken," said Matokuwapi. The elk held his head high. "This land belongs to me!"

"To you?" scoffed Tatanka as he flexed the strong muscles on his back. "What gives you the right to claim this land?"

"It's simple," Matokuwapi bellowed. "I got here first. Now everything belongs to me."

"It isn't simple at all," Tatanka responded. "I have looked at this place for many years from High Mountain. I saw it before you did."

"This is mine," Matokuwapi continued, pushing Tatanka away.

"It belongs to me," said Tatanka. He smashed his antlers against Matokuwapi's with a loud crash.

Day after day, they argued and pushed and shoved. The crash of antlers echoed throughout the valley. Nostrils flared; eyes glared. The elks trampled the grass and knocked down new trees. The valley filled with the noise of their fighting.

One day, a crow descended from the blue sky. "What's all this ruckus?" he asked.

"Tell this elk to get off my land," Matokuwapi said.

"It's *my* land," Tatanka disagreed.

"Stop!" said the crow. "Let the Monarch decide. She is a wise judge."

Matokuwapi and Tatanka were exhausted, so they agreed. Besides, Matokuwapi was sure the Monarch would rule for him. Tatanka had no doubt that he would win.

"Go to the stream at the far end of the valley," the crow said. "The Monarch will find you there."

As tired as they were, Matokuwapi and Tatanka walked slowly to the stream. No sooner had they arrived when they heard the gentle flapping of wings. An orange-and-black butterfly fluttered overhead, then alighted on a peach blossom.

"I am the Monarch," the butterfly said. "What is the problem?"

First Matokuwapi made his claim. Then Tatanka made his argument. The judge closed her eyes as she listened intently.

"I understand your reasoning, Elk Matokuwapi," the butterfly said. "You make an excellent case for it."

Matokuwapi's eyes lit up. He was sure he had won.

"But," the judge continued, "Elk Tatanka, your logic is equally good."

Tatanka's chest swelled with pride. He looked at Matokuwapi smugly.

"There is only one way to settle this quarrel," said the butterfly. "I want you to return together to the disputed land just before sunrise. Don't utter a word when you get there. Don't argue or fight. Just listen. Then you will hear the decision." The Monarch then stretched her wings over her head and flew away.

Early the next morning, Tatanka and Matokuwapi met in the valley. The sky was dark and everything was silent. It was difficult, but they held their tongues.

Matokuwapi and Tatanka waited eagerly. Finally they heard a faint whisper from the ground.

"Do you hear that?" Matokuwapi asked.

"*Sshh,*" Tatanka said.

The elk tilted their heads and pressed their ears close to the ground. The whisper came again. It was the voice of the Earth.

"Both of you belong to me," the Earth said. "Both of you belong to me."

Some things must be shared in order to be enjoyed. What do you think Matokuwapi and Tatanka will have to do to get along with each other?

Riverside

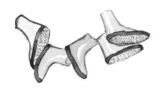

Zimena decided to spend a lazy day in the country. She brought eight rubber boots to keep her spidery feet from getting muddy and packed a poncho in case it rained. She stuffed crumbs of vanilla biscuits into her pockets, then headed out of town.

"Here is a quiet place for a picnic," Zimena thought. She ran down a steep path to the edge of the river. Quickly pulling off her boots, she spread her poncho on the ground. She listened to the wind rustling tulip leaves while she munched on her snack.

Zimena was sunning her purply self and was nearly asleep when she heard a cry.

"Help! Please help!" called a tiny spider bobbing up and down in the water.

"Oh my!" Zimena gasped. She quickly spun and cast a silky net into the water. The helpless creature grabbed the web and Zimena dragged him to safety.

"Are you all right?" Zimena asked as she freed the spider from the sticky threads.

"Yes, yes," he said, shivering with cold and fright. Before she could say another word, he ran upstream. "Thanks!" he yelled over his shoulders.

Zimena returned to her pleasant tasks of sunning and thinking and eating crumbs. Suddenly she heard a second voice calling for help. She looked up and saw another spider in the swirling water. Again she spun a web, cast it into the river, and pulled out the second soaking spider.

"Are you okay?" Zimena puffed. She was getting tired.

"A little scared, that's all. Thanks for saving me," the rescued spider said and ran upstream.

Zimena settled herself once more and was enjoying her cookie crumbs when she again heard cries for help and saw eight hairy arms waving above the water. Again she came to the rescue.

Zimena was exhausted from spinning webs and pulling drowning spiders from the river.

"I can't do this anymore," Zimena panted. "I have to see what is going on."

So she went upstream. Around the bend, she saw a group of spiders. One spider was standing on a ledge that jutted out over the swift river. Zimena realized what he was about to do. "Wait!" she shouted. "Why are you jumping into the river?"

"We need to get to the other side," the spider explained. The current is strong and many of us can't swim against it, but we must try."

Zimena thought about how much she wanted to sit by herself and munch on crumbs. Then she thought about the drowning spiders. Finally she asked, "Can you spin webs?" They all answered that they could.

"Then watch me." Zimena crawled up a tree trunk and out on a limb that hung over the water. Then she leaped from branch to branch, weaving a bridge behind her until she reached the other side.

Zimena returned to the spiders. "You can spin a web like that, too," she said. "I'll teach you."

So Zimena and the other spiders spent the morning building bridges together—spidery, silky bridges. Now they could cross rivers, little and big, whenever they wanted.

Zimena could enjoy her day at last.

She returned to her quiet place and, looking up at the cloudless sky, sang to no one in particular. Then she put her hand into the pockets of her poncho and finally finished her vanilla biscuits.

We sometimes are called upon to help those we don't know. Why do you think Zimena came to the rescue of the drowning spiders?

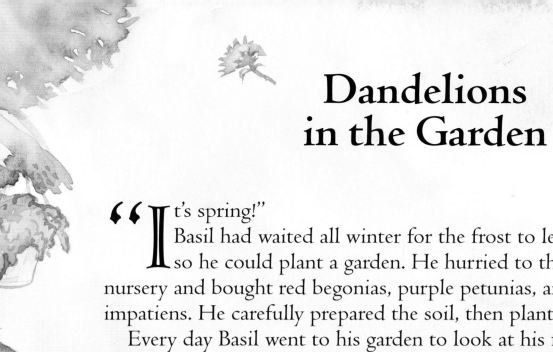

Dandelions
in the Garden

"It's spring!"

Basil had waited all winter for the frost to leave the earth so he could plant a garden. He hurried to the garden nursery and bought red begonias, purple petunias, and white impatiens. He carefully prepared the soil, then planted his seedlings.

Every day Basil went to his garden to look at his flowers. The garden overflowed with colors — red, purple and white — exactly as he had dreamed.

But one day, Basil found something unexpected.

"Dandelion weeds!" he said in dismay.

Basil hadn't planted dandelions and he didn't want them — with their yellow petals and their spiky green leaves. He wanted only red begonias, purple petunias, and white impatiens. So he used a trowel to dig up every weed he could find.

"It is a pretty garden indeed," Basil said as he enjoyed his flowers.

The next day, when Basil went out to admire his garden, he saw that the dandelions had returned. He talked to his neighbor about what to do.

"If you really want to get rid of them, you have to keep after them," Brunhilda said. "Dig them out as soon as you can."

Each day, Basil crouched in his garden and crept on his knees. As soon as the first dandelion poked through the soil, he attacked it. But every time he went to his garden, he discovered more dandelions. He gave up his trowel and used a shovel. But still the dandelions grew.

He pulled and plucked them, pinched and plowed them, snipped and yanked them. No matter what he did, the dandelions kept coming back — every day, more dandelions.

Once again, Basil went to Brunhilda.

"You have to try harder," Brunhilda advised. "If you really don't want them, you mustn't give up."

Basil decided that from then on he would sleep in the garden. He would catch the dandelions the moment they broke through the soil! But the giraffe soon grew tired. He fell asleep with his head against the fence. When the sun rose, Basil jumped to his feet and scoured the garden. He pulled a dandelion here, he pulled a dandelion there until he was exhausted. Basil was so tired that his midday nap stretched into his nighttime sleep.

The next morning Basil followed the same routine. But no matter what he did and no matter how hard he tried, he couldn't completely rid the garden of dandelions. One red begonia, one dandelion. One purple petunia, one dandelion. One white impatiens, one dandelion.

"What do I do now?" he asked Brunhilda

"There is only one thing left to do," she said. "I suggest that you learn to love dandelions."

"But I want flowers, not weeds," Basil complained. He thought that Brunhilda was teasing him.

"A weed is only a name that we give to an unloved flower," Brunhilda continued. "You don't have to rid your garden of all the dandelions. Indeed, a few dandelions will make your garden even more beautiful."

Basil thought about what Brunhilda said as he returned to his garden. He looked at his flowers: red begonias, purple petunias, and white impatiens. And then he could see the dandelions were flowers, too.

From then on, Basil made sure that each flower had its proper place and, just as Brunhilda had predicted, he enjoyed his garden more than ever: a garden of red begonias, purple petunias, white impatiens, and yellow dandelions.

Many things are beautiful. Why do you think Basil didn't find dandelions beautiful at first?

Lola and the Caged Bird

Every Friday morning Lola went to the Bird Market where she saw hundreds of birds in their cages. She enjoyed listening to the calls of sparrows and nightingales, meadowlarks, and bright yellow canaries.

One day, above all the chirping and chattering of the hundreds of birds, she heard a beautiful song. Lola looked up and there in a golden cage was a bird she did not recognize.

"I see you admire the bird," the birdseller said to Lola.

"Yes, oh, yes," Lola said breathlessly. "What kind is it?"

"In fact, I don't know, madam," the birdseller said. "I just received the bird this morning. I have never seen another like it before."

"It is gorgeous!" Lola said.

"What's more," the birdseller added, "I was told there is no other bird like it anywhere in the world. So, would you like to buy it?"

Lola couldn't resist. Although she had never bought a bird before, she took out her wallet and paid the birdseller the price he asked.

Lola returned home a very happy elephant. In her hand she held the golden cage, and in the cage was the most resplendent bird anyone had ever seen.

The bird added great happiness to Lola's life. In the morning, the bird sang the sweetest song as Lola ate her breakfast. When she returned home from work in the evening, Lola's heart leaped with the thrill of seeing such a thing of beauty.

Lola took great care that the bird always had enough water and seed. She cleaned the cage every day and placed it on her balcony so the bird would have sunlight and fresh air.

Months passed. Then one day Lola realized that the bird's melody wasn't as sweet as it once had been. There was now something slightly melancholy in its tune. Lola noticed that the beautiful colors had begun to fade — the red feathers had become pink, the green ones had turned to dark gray, and the yellows had lost their brightness. Each day the bird became duller and duller.

Lola was overcome with sadness as she watched the bird whither away.

"I don't know what more I can do for you," she said to the bird.

Through her sobs Lola heard a small sound.

"On the other side of the ocean," the bird whispered, "is another bird much like me."

Lola couldn't believe her ears.

"I thought you were the only one in the world," she said.

"There is another," said the bird. "Find it. It will tell you what to do."

So Lola set out to cross the sea. She looked along the Malabar coast but saw nothing like her bird. She searched the Irrawady Delta but heard no song that was as beautiful. She scoured the plains of Tibet and the cliffsides of the Himalayan Mountains, but to no avail.

Lola was ready to give up her quest when she heard a sound coming from the leafy canopy of a rain forest in Borneo. It was the same song her bird sang.

Lola gasped. For here was a bird that looked exactly like the bird she had bought. It shimmered with bright and beautiful colors and it filled the forest with song.

Lola put out her hand and the bird alighted upon her palm.

"I must talk to you," she said. She told her sad story and asked the bird for advice.

The bird said to her, "When you are happy, you are beautiful. But you can't be happy when you are in a cage. A prison is a prison, even if it is made of gold. You must open the door to the cage and set your bird free."

Lola's heart nearly broke when she heard this. Tears ran down her cheeks. She sat quietly thinking on a tree stump for several minutes.

"Yes, yes," she finally said, wiping away her tears with her trunk. "I know you are right. I must go home before it is too late."

When Lola returned, she did exactly as she had been told.

"I am sorry, dear bird," she said.

With that, the bird flew away, its feathers growing brighter in the sunshine. It flew until it disappeared over the hillside, leaving behind a dazzling rainbow that faded only when the sun set.

What makes one happy may not bring happiness to another. Do you think Lola was happy or sad to see her bird fly away?

Passing Through a Gate

Nicholas and his son Victor had quite a reputation in the town of Bishkek. Camels everywhere are known for their contrariness — they knock into things without warning and stop just as abruptly, sleep when they want even if it means standing up, and sit on rocks or sand or sofas as they please. But there wasn't a camel in the world that compared to these two. They were considered stubborn even by other camels.

Everywhere he went, Nicholas wore a pink-and-orange bow tie with a T-shirt. Victor ate avocado and mayonnaise spread on his apricot salad, even though not a single camel had eaten such a dish since last year. The two of them once put on overcoats in the summer just because that was what their camelly selves wanted to do.

One day, as Nicholas was walking around in circles even though it must have been a hundred degrees out, he received a letter.

"This is good news, Victor," the camel announced as he read the letter. "Tomorrow your Aunt Tamisha is arriving from Alma-Ata. I haven't seen my sister in years."

Victor couldn't contain his excitement. The two humps on his back quivered like palm leaves in the wind. Aunt Tamisha, his very favorite relative, was coming to visit.

Victor loved Aunt Tamisha because she always laughed at his jokes. She also went everywhere with an umbrella and Victor thought this was the most interesting thing any camel could do.

"How long will she be staying?" the young camel asked.

"She is on her way to Tashkent," his father said, "so she can only stay for a short while. A few hours, I'm afraid."

Early the next morning Nicholas sent Victor to an oasis several miles away to gather fruits and nuts for Aunt Tamisha.

"Don't delay," Nicholas called after his son. "Hurry back so you'll have time to spend with your aunt."

Victor rushed to the trees around the watering hole, picked dates and almonds, and began to trot back to Bishkek. He had plenty of time left to see his aunt.

Just as he was about to pass through the city's narrow gate, he had the misfortune to meet Urgut, a camel nearly as strong-headed as he. Urgut was just about ready to pass through the gate to leave the city and Victor was about ready to enter.

"Let me pass," Victor said to Urgut, who stood there blocking the way. The gate was wide enough for only one camel to pass through at a time.

Urgut refused to let Victor pass first and Victor wouldn't step aside for Urgut.

"I'm in a hurry to see my aunt, Urgut," Victor explained. "She is visiting today. She is staying for only a few hours. So get out of my way!"

"No, no, no, no, and no," the other camel grunted. "You move out of my way and let me pass first."

"I was here before you," Victor replied. "So get out of *my* way."

"Actually, I was here before you," Urgut insisted. "*You* have to move for *me*." The two of them stood there, nose-to-nose under the stone archway, as obstinate as only two camels can be.

Meanwhile, Aunt Tamisha had indeed arrived at Nicholas's home.

"Where is my nephew Victor?" Tamisha asked as she drank a cup of tea mixed with yak butter and salt.

"I don't know what is keeping that boy," Victor's father said. "It's getting late. I'll go find him."

"Please hurry," Tamisha said. "I have to leave soon."

When Nicholas reached the city gate, he found his way blocked by Urgut. He could see Victor standing on the other side, his hooves dug deep in the earth, the dust deeper than his ankles.

"Let my son pass," Nicholas told Urgut.

"He'll go as soon as I pass," Urgut called over his shoulder to Nicholas.

Urgut then looked straight at Victor. While Urgut's back was turned, Nicholas got on his knees and quickly crawled through the other camel's legs to reach his son.

"You go home now to see your aunt," Nicholas said to Victor. "I'll stand here in your place."

So Victor sucked in his breath and made himself skinny enough to sneak past Urgut, who was now so busy keeping Nicholas from passing through the gate that he hardly noticed.

Victor ran as fast as he could, his humps bouncing from side to side.

"Auntie, Auntie Tamisha!" he called as he approached his home. But his aunt had already taken the early train to Tashkent. Victor threw himself on the sand and cried.

Victor's father remained at the gate for the rest of the day. Finally, when the sun set behind the dunes, Urgut said to Nicholas, "Oh, all right. I've had enough."

"Aha, I've won!" Nicholas snorted.

Urgut stepped aside and let him pass. Nicholas ran home as fast as he could, his two humps bouncing from side to side.

Of course, when Nicholas reached home, he discovered that Tamisha was gone. And there was Victor, fast asleep under a silk umbrella that Tamisha had left for him as a present.

Sometimes being stubborn can cause unhappiness. What do you think Victor could have done instead of standing at the gate for so long?

Black or White All Over

Where the sky is wide and the wild grass grows the color of honey, hundreds and hundreds of animals graze on the rich earth. There are big animals that scoop water with long noses and tall creatures with necks so long that they eat leaves from the treetops.

Once four-legged creatures with stripes on their heads and backs and legs lived on one side of this beautiful plain. On the other side was another herd of four-legged creatures who also had stripes all over their bodies.

While these two groups lived close to each other — only a gallop away — they kept a good distance between them.

One day while he was grazing with his family, a stallion lifted his head from the grass and spoke to his son.

"Punda," the stallion said, "there are some things you need to know. We are special animals. These magnificent black stripes on our white bodies are beautiful beyond compare."

And one day while she was grazing with her family, a mare from the other herd lifted her head from the grass and spoke to her daughter.

"Milia," the mare said, "there are some things you must learn. What makes us special are these beautiful white stripes that we wear across our black coats. None can compare to us."

All year long, Punda grazed with his herd. Soon he was big enough to walk away a little by himself.

Milia, too, had grown enough to wander alone.

One day the two animals rounded a corner and came face-to-face. Never had Punda seen such a beautiful beast as the one before his eyes. And Milia's heart beat quickly with the sight of the lovely creature in front of her.

The two talked and played, then galloped home so fast a plume of dust rose to the blue sky. Both were eager to tell their parents about the love they had found.

"I found the most beautiful mare today," Punda said to his father.

But when his father learned where she came from, he said, "No, Punda. This isn't right. You shouldn't see her again."

"Why do you say that?" Punda asked, surprised.

"It's obvious, Punda," his father tried to explain. "You only have to look at her."

"I did look at her and I think she's beautiful," said Punda.

"Not at all," the father persisted. "She is too different — she is ugly. After all, she is black with white stripes and we are white with black stripes."

Meanwhile, at her home, Milia told her mother about Punda.

"He is the most wonderful colt in all the world," said Milia.

But when her mother discovered where he came from, she said, "No, Milia. This isn't right. You shouldn't see him again."

Milia wanted to know why.

"It's obvious," Milia's mother tried to explain. "He is white with black stripes and not at all like us. We are black with white stripes."

Punda and Milia didn't know what to do. Sad and heartbroken, they kept apart for many days.

Then one day Punda and Milia arrived at the watering hole at the same time. At first they thought they would run away. But their happiness at seeing each other overcame their fear and they embraced. They spent the rest of the day together, grazing on the wild grass and playing in the shadows of the snow-covered mountain.

Punda and Milia grew older and continued to see each other, always in secret. Finally they went off to begin a family of their own. Their parents vowed never to see them again.

When the young couple had their first foal, no one could tell whether the baby was white and black or black and white. The same was true when they had more colts and fillies.

Punda's and Milia's parents heard about the babies and their hearts broke at the thought of not seeing their grandchildren. They decided that it was now time to pay a visit.

Punda and Milia were surprised, but above all, they were profoundly happy.

"I want to apologize to you," Punda's father said.

"And I do, too," said Milia's mother.

"We are glad that you've come," Punda said with great joy.

"Here are your grandchildren," Milia said as she introduced the little ones.

The grandparents had tears in their eyes as they kissed each grandchild.

From that day on, all of the zebras from both herds became friends. Today no one can remember why they hadn't liked each other. It all seems so long ago.

Everyone can make mistakes. Why do you think Punda's and Milia's parents didn't want their son and daughter to see each other?

About the Author

As the Leader of the Ethical Humanist Society of Long Island since 1968 and advisor to the Sunday School and youth group, ARTHUR DOBRIN has many years of experience teaching morals and values. The stories in this collection have been told to countless Sunday School children.

Born in Brooklyn, New York, Dr. Dobrin received a masters degree in human relations from New York University and a doctorate in social welfare from Adelphi University's School of Social Work. He has frequently traveled to Kenya in East Africa, where he and his wife served in the Peace Corps.

Dr. Dobrin is a professor of humanities and social sciences at Hofstra University's New College and a cofounder of the Long Island Interracial Alliance for a Common Future. He holds a certificate in family psychotherapy from the Ackerman Family Institute in New York. Dr. Dobrin has three grown children and two grandchildren and lives with his wife in Westbury, New York.

About the Artist

JACQUELINE ROGERS was born and raised in Connecticut and is a graduate of the Rhode Island School of Design. Other books she has illustrated for Scholastic include *Ballerina Dreams*; *A Boy Named Boomer*; *Snow Angel*; *Five Live Bongos*; *Monster Soup and Other Spooky Poems*; and *Best Friends Sleep Over*, which she also wrote.

Ms. Rogers lives in upstate New York and has two young daughters.